CW00840478

First published in 1974 by
Dean, an imprint of
The Hamlyn Publishing Group Limited
Michelin House, 81 Fulham Road, London SW3 6RB
This reprint 1992
Text and illustrations Copyright © Deans International
Publishing, a division of The Hamlyn Publishing Group Limited 1974

ISBN 0 603 01235 3

Printed in Great Britain

TED'S HELICOPTER

Written and Illustrated
by
VIOLET M. WILLIAMS

ONE sunny day Ted was dozing beneath a tree when he was wakened up by a loud buzzing, whirring sort of noise.

It came from above Ted's head and when he looked up to see what it was he could hardly believe his eyes.

"What a strange bird!" he gasped. "I must go and ask clever Alan Owl what kind it is."

Ted ran along so fast to

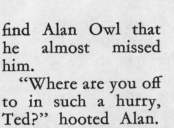

find Alan Owl that he almost missed him.

"Where are you off to in such a hurry, Ted?" hooted Alan.

"I am looking for *you*!" cried Ted. "Did you see that funny bird?"

Then he caught his toe on a big stone and fell.

The teddy bear lost his hat as he landed at the feet of his friend, Bruce Bun.

"Where did you come from?" asked Bruce, in surprise. "You seemed to fall out of the sky!"

That reminded Ted why he was in such a hurry.

"I was looking for Alan," he replied. "As he is a bird himself I thought he would know what kind of bird flies with a whirring and a buzzing noise."

"Of course I know," said Alan, flying up. "I am sure, well almost sure, that it was a—er—a—"

"You do *not* know," put in Pamela Piglet, who had just trotted along with Serena Squirrel.

"It was not a bird at all," said Serena Squirrel. Everyone stared at Serena.

"Come home with me and I will show you," she told them.

Serena had a picture-book of AEROPLANES. She had found it at the foot of her tree-house and she had looked at every page.

"It was a HELICOPTER!" she said, showing Ted a picture of one.

When Ted lifted his nose out of the book he sighed.

"I *would* like to fly!" he said, longingly.

Bruce's brother tried to float off with the help of a big balloon, but didn't get far.

"We will *make* a helicopter," cried Ted.

Bruce and his brother and even Serena said that they would help. They sawed and screwed and knocked and glued to make a helicopter out of wood.

The friends did not know what to use for the whirring blades which would twist around and help the helicopter to fly.

"I have three big paper fans," said Serena.

The fans were fastened into place and the helicopter or, rather, the TEDICOPTER, was ready to try out.

Bruce and Serena held it up and Alan flew in front to show how flying was done, but the helicopter would not take off.

Soon Bruce and Serena could not hold up the home-made helicopter any longer and down it fell.

"What *are* you trying to do, Ted?" asked Mortimer, a friendly magician who lived nearby.

"We have made a Tedicopter," said Ted. "But it won't fly like a helicopter."

"I am not surprised," grinned Mortimer. "It has to have an engine and things that you cannot make."

"Then we will have

to give up," sighed Ted.

"Such hard work deserves some return," smiled Mortimer. "I will help."

SWOOSH!

That SWOOSH was the Tedicopter swishing up into the air. How it had changed!

Now it was bright pink and blue, with a pretty flower painted on the side. It had twisting and twirling blades which carried it even faster than Alan's wings carried *him*.

When the helicopter came down to earth again the big curved front window shot open as if by magic, which, of course, it was; *Mortimer's* magic!

Ted could hardly wait to scramble inside. He was so excited that he did not even notice that the white flower was a big surprised EYE!

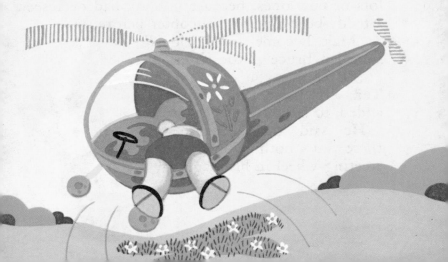

Ted had a wonderful time flying over the countryside. He waved to old friends and he made lots of new ones, because nobody had ever seen a teddy-bear flying a helicopter before.

"May I come for a ride?" squealed Bruce's little sister.

"Of course you can!" yelled Ted. "IF I can get down," he added, to himself.

He said that because there was nothing but a steering-wheel in his magic

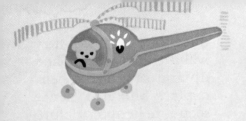

helicopter and he
did not know *what*
to do to GET
down!

But no sooner
had Ted thought that he would *like* to go down
than DOWN the helicopter began to take him!

Bruce, Serena and Pamela were waiting for him.
"Please will you take *us* for a ride?" they asked.

"Climb in!" beamed Ted.

Somehow they all fitted in, and that must have
been Mortimer's magic again!

Ellie Elephant
lived in
the Zoo
and she
was taking

one of her country walks when she looked up and saw Ted's helicopter. She had never seen a helicopter before and she stared up at it in great surprise.

"Let us go down and let Ellie see my Tedi copter," said Ted, wanting to show off a little.

The helicopter was being very good and as soon as it heard this it swooshed down towards Ellie.

Ellie had never seen anything like the helicopter before

and she stood watching it come lower and lower.

At first she thought she had better run away and she got ready to hold on her woolly hat. She always wore a woolly hat or a woolly scarf because she came from a hotter country than this one, and today she was wearing both.

Then she decided to meet this

strange flying thing face-to-face and so she bravely set off towards it.

Alan Owl kindly flew down to explain the Tedicopter to Ellie and he rested on her back.

"No doubt you do not know what that strange thing is," he began. "It is called a—er—a—"

Alan had forgotten again but it did not matter as Ellie was going to see for herself.

She trotted across the grass and along the path so fast that her hat blew off and —Alan fell off, too! He shot over Ellie's head and landed on the path just as Ted and his friends came down to earth.

"How clever of you to make a helicopter," said Ellie, when she heard the story.

The helicopter frowned when Ted forgot to mention Mortimer's magic help.

The helicopter was very cross when Ted said that Ellie could come for a ride with the rest of them!

Ellie could not squeeze into the helicopter, though she tried hard. "I will have to ride on the tail," she puffed, trying to climb on to it.

"Not on MY tail you will not!" thought the poor helicopter.

Elephants are so BIG!

Ellie did her best to ride on the helicopter's tail but it would not take off with her there. "It is tired, poor thing," she said kindly. "*I* will give *it* a ride, for a change!"

And be-fore the Tedicopter knew what

was happening it was on Ellie's back, being carried along at a brisk trot!

"This IS nice!" it beamed.

"Now I am an ELLIE-COPTER!" giggled Ellie.

Ellie carried everyone to the Zoo Keeper's cottage where they were all invited in for tea.

"It is fun having a helicopter," said Ted. "But I think I would rather ride on Ellie's nice safe back!"

The Ted-Ellie-Helicopter heard that and it gave a sigh of relief.

"In that case I will go and find another friendly helicopter," it decided. And off it went, taking Alan for a joy-ride. That was something Alan had never had before and he boasted about it FOREVER!